For the hearts that bent when breaking felt easier.
For the parents who wished their words had come sooner.
For the children who waited for gentleness.
For those who left, and those who found their way back.
And for the flowers that bloom long after the cold is gone.

PROLOGUE
Before Anything Blooms

Before the story begins, the garden rests.

At the edge of the village, an old stone cottage stood
behind a garden that had long stopped waiting for
anyone. Ivy curled around the walls like memories that
refused to loosen their grip. The shrubs had grown
thick and uneven, leaning into one another as though
seeking comfort in their neglect. An ancient rosebush,
once carefully tended, now reached its branches
toward the back window like a plea for someone to
remember it.

Inside the cottage lived Peter Whitfield, a man who
had grown accustomed to silence. His steps were
slow, his routines steady, his days built around the
kind of quiet that settles when life has been both
loved and lost. He carried his past without complaint,
the way one carries an old injury, aware of it in every
movement, though rarely speaking its name.

Most mornings, just before the sun stretched over the
fields, Peter paused at the back door. He liked to
pretend he was studying the weather or checking if the
stone path had shifted again. But deep down, beneath
the habits taught long ago, he knew better.

He was searching for something he had not felt in
years.

A sign.

A softness.

A reason to believe that life still held a place for him.

Once, he had loved easily. Once, he had laughed without measuring who might hear. But loss had a way of teaching caution, and grief had taught him silence far more deeply than his father's book ever had.
That book still sat on the highest shelf.
Leather worn.
Spine cracked.
Its pages filled with rules that had shaped him long before he had the courage to question them.

Strength is built through silence. Emotion is an indulgence of the weak.

He no longer believed those words, yet they clung to him like old shadows. Even now, he lived half in the world his father had built and half in the one he no longer knew how to enter.
Then, one cold winter morning when frost lay over the garden like a breath held too long, the quite shifted.
A knock.
Soft.
Uneven.
But certain.
Peter opened the door to find a young woman on the step, her cheeks flushed from the cold, her coat dusted with snow. She looked at him with a steady kindness that felt foreign and familiar all at once.
"Mr Whitfield?" she asked.
Her voice was gentle.
Her presence even gentler.
Her name was Rose Bennett.

And although neither of them could have known it then, her arrival would become the first small crack in the wall around Peter's life, the kind that lets light through.

When she stepped inside, bringing warmth with her, something in the neglected garden behind the cottage seemed to shift.

As though the earth paused.

Listened.

And prepared, in its quiet way, for spring.

CHAPTER ONE
The Visitor

—————————◆—————————

The kettle reached its boil with a low, irritated rumble, as though annoyed at having to perform the same task every morning. Peter Whitfield heard it from his chair but made no move to rise. He sat in the worn armchair by the narrow window, his hands resting lightly on the wooden arms polished by decades of habit. Outside, a faint mist clung to the fields, softening the outline of the distant hedgerows.

The cottage was small, but its beams and stone floors hinted at age and craftsmanship. Peter kept it tidy, though sparsely furnished, his possessions arranged with the precision of a man who no longer wished to own more than he needed. And yet here and there, contradiction seeped in a handwoven Persian rug with reds that still glowed as though lit from within; a tall clock whose brass pendulum swung with an elegance that suggested it had once presided over an entrance hall far grander than this cottage's.

He had money. More than the village suspected. But simplicity felt like penance.

A knock came, not tentative, but confident. Three lively taps.

Peter stiffened. He recognised that pattern.

"Come in," he called, without raising his voice.

The door opened and sunlight seemed to tumble in with the figure in navy scrubs. Richard, his community nurse, entered with the bright air of someone who found life consistently pleasing and saw no reason to hide it.

"Good morning, Peter!" he said, shrugging off his jacket. "Just look at that sky. Quite deceptive really. Makes promises it's not going to keep."

Peter watched him move about the cottage as if it were his own, checking the counters, glancing at the half-empty tea tin, nudging the kettle. Richard's presence filled the space in a way that felt both intrusive and oddly reassuring.

"You're early," Peter said.

"Am I? My watch says ten-thirty." Richard squinted. "Which means I'm late. As usual. Don't tell my supervisor."

"I don't know your supervisor."

"And they don't know you, which makes this a perfect arrangement."

Richard turned the kettle back on.

"You haven't eaten, have you?"

"I have."

Richard's eyes glanced briefly toward the lone, untouched slice of toast on the counter.

"Ah," he said, in a tone that accepted the lie without approving it. "Very filling, I'm sure."

He prepared the tea, moving with an ease that suggested he had been doing this for a long time, not only in households like Peter's but with people who had grown used to hiding their frailty. He handed Peter a mug with a small flourish.

"There we go. A little warmth."

"Thank you," Peter said quietly.

Richard settled into the chair opposite him, crossing his legs and balancing a clipboard on his knee. "Now then. How are we this morning? Feeling dizzy? Achy? Existentially troubled?"

"Alive."

"I'll put that under 'stable.'"
Richard wrapped the blood pressure cuff around
Peter's arm.
"You're quieter than usual," he said.
"You say that every visit."
"And every time it's true. But today feels different. A
bit heavier."
Peter kept his gaze on the window.
"There are mornings when memories surface whether
you invite them or not."
"Good ones or bad?"
"Both," Peter murmured. "The problem is that the
good ones hurt more."
Richard stayed silent long enough for the machine to
finish its reading.
"Your blood pressure's tad high," he said gently.
"Anything worrying you?"
"Nothing I can change."
Richard scribbled something. "You're too cryptic for
your own good, Peter."
The old man's eyes drifted toward the mantel. A glass
dome sat there, housing a rare gold watch with a map
engraved on its face. The watch had belonged to his
father. It was worth a small fortune. But Peter never
wore it. Couldn't bear to.
Richard followed his gaze. "You keep that thing
polished. Why not wear it?"
"Some things are better kept as reminders," Peter said.
"Of what?"
Peter did not answer.
The nurse shifted, unsure whether to push.
The silence stretched between them, long and fine like
a thread pulled between two distant points. It was
Richard who finally broke it.

"I talk too much, you know," he said lightly. "My sister says I'm exhausting. She says I expend the energy of three human beings before lunchtime."
Peter almost, almost, smiled. "Yes."
Richard laughed, pleased by the faint humour. "See? You're not hopeless. Buried under all that gloom is a man with a sense of humour."
Peter looked at him, then looked away.
"You remind me of someone."
"Oh? Someone cheerful and handsome, I hope."
"Someone who talked too much," Peter said.
Richard put a hand dramatically to his heart.
"Flattered." Peter did not respond, but something in his eyes softened, the smallest fracture in an otherwise rigid expression.

CHAPTER TWO
The Whitfield Manor

The smell of icing always brought it back. In the old manor's kitchen, little Peter, no more than seven, stood on a wooden stool to reach the counter. His mother, apron tied over her elegant dress, scooped frosting from a bowl and swirled it over a towering cake decorated with real flowers.

"There," she said. "What do you think?"

"It's beautiful," Peter said honestly.

She pressed a dab of icing on his nose. "You're not supposed to say that. You're supposed to say, 'I'll wait until the guests taste it.'"

Peter wiped his nose, giggling.

"Is Father coming to the party?"

His mother paused, barely a heartbeat, but long enough for Peter to notice.

"He said he will."

That didn't answer the question.

Servants bustled around them, setting dishes, polishing silver, adjusting ribbons. Chandeliers sparkled overhead. The manor was a kingdom of marble floors, carved fireplaces, and long hallways lined with portraits of stern Whitfields from centuries past.

A footman passed by with a tray of decorated biscuits. "Happy birthday, Master Peter."

Peter gave a shy nod. "Thank you."

His mother leaned close. "Go on, explore. See if your friends from town have arrived yet."

He hopped off the stool, eager, but before he could take two steps, a deep voice called his name from the entrance of the kitchen.

"Peter."

He felt the excitement drain from his chest.

His father, Raymond Whitfield, stood in the doorway. Tall, broad-shouldered, impeccably groomed. His face bore no softness. His presence wrapped the room in a quiet tension.

"Come with me," Raymond said.

Peter followed his father down the long corridor, the walls crowded with artefacts collected from years of travel, painted masks with fixed expressions, carved figures, rolled maps, globes with faded oceans. Peter had always been drawn to them, imagining the places they came from. But he knew better than to ask. His father disliked questions almost as much as he disliked interruptions.

In the study, the heavy oak door closed with a dull thud behind them. Raymond Whitfield crossed over to a tall mahogany shelf crowded with maps, statuettes, and polished trophies from distant corners of the world. From the highest row he drew out a book Peter had never seen before. Its spine was cracked, its corners worn soft with age.

Raymond turned, studying him.

"Seven today," he said.

"Yes, Father."

"You're growing. Soon you'll be expected to conduct yourself as a Whitfield ought to."

Peter straightened automatically.

"Birthdays," Raymond continued, "are unnecessary displays. Your mother insisted on this one, so you will behave accordingly. No tears. No outbursts. No foolish excitement."

Peter hesitated. "Excited? But I …"

"Do not interrupt."

Peter's mouth closed at once.

"Emotion," his father said, "is a liability. Sentiment clouds judgment. You will not indulge it."

Peter swallowed. "I don't understand."

"You don't need to understand. You need to obey." Raymond held out the book. His voice shifted, becoming formal in a way that made Peter's skin prickle.

"This belonged to your grandfather," he said. "It contains the Whitfield lineage and the principles that built everything you see. Read it. Learn from it. And remember it."

Peter took the book carefully.

Inside, the pages were filled with tight, looping handwriting. Diagrams of trade routes. Ledger examples. Short, rigid rules written like commandments.

He paused over one line:

"Strength is built through silence. Emotion is an indulgence of the weak."

Raymond tapped the page.

"That is what it means to be a Whitfield."

Peter nodded, not yet understanding how those words would mould him.

He would keep the book for decades, not because he believed in its teachings, but because it was the only thing his father had ever given him freely.

When he returned to the kitchen, his mother touched
Peter's cheek gently.
"You alright, darling?"
Peter nodded. He was starting to hide his feelings
without meaning to.
His mother knelt and smoothed his hair. "You don't
need to stop feeling things. You hear me?"
He looked at her. "Father says…"
"Your father," she interrupted gently, "expects too
much of someone so small."
She hugged him, and he clung to her, hiding his face
in her shoulder.
On that birthday, Peter learned that love and
obedience could point in different directions.
And that he would spend his life walking between
them.

CHAPTER THREE
Rules of a Whitfield

Young Peter learned the rules early.
Rule One:
Do not show emotion.
Rule Two:
Work precedes everything.
Rule Three:
Your future is a legacy, not a choice.
Rule Four:
The world respects strength, not affection.

The manor echoed with these laws. His father's footsteps carried them. The servants moved as though governed by them. Even the artefacts on the walls seemed to embody them, proud, cold, detached. Peter learned to swallow laughter. He learned not to cry even when he fell from a horse and tore open his knee. He learned to sit stiffly with his father in the study, memorising numbers and trade routes while longing to run outside with his friends.
His mother was the only rebellion against his father's empire of silence. She sang in the mornings.
She told stories at night. She whispered kindness into the cracks that formed in Peter's small heart.
And because of that, he adored her.
But the rules of a Whitfield were heavier than childhood affection.
When guests arrived, his father introduced Peter as "the next Whitfield."
Not as a boy.

Not as a son.

As an heir.

Peter forced a polite smile and stood quietly beside him.

Inside, he felt small.

CHAPTER FOUR
A Boy of Two Worlds

The estate grounds stretched across rolling fields.
There were horses, stables, dogs, formal gardens, and
ancient trees that had seen more Whitfields come and
go than any family record could list.
Peter loved exploring the grounds with a wooden
sword and a sense of adventure.
His mother encouraged these secret escapades.
"You're allowed to be young," she whispered.
"Don't let him take that from you."
They would walk the gardens together, her hand warm
around his.
But his father disapproved of such frivolity.
"This estate exists because Whitfields worked," he
said. "Not because they played."
Peter learned to hide his joy.
To tuck his laughter away.
To show his mother his true self only when they were
alone.
And always, beneath everything, he felt guilty for not
being the son his father wanted.

CHAPTER FIVE
The End of Warmth

His mother's illness came quietly.
A slow waning of colour.
A tremble in her hands.
A cough that lingered.
The doctors came often.
They were polite, but their eyes avoided Peter's.
One winter evening, the doctor stepped out of her room with a heavy sigh.
"She's asking for you," he told Peter softly.
Peter slipped inside.
His mother lay in the large four-poster bed, covered in quilts that once warmed her laughter-filled mornings.
She reached for his hand.
"My darling," she whispered, brushing her thumb against his cheek. "I want you to remember something."
Peter's voice cracked. "I will."
"You are allowed to feel," she said. "You are allowed to love."
"I do," he whispered. "I love you."
She smiled. "And that is your strength."
Moments later, she closed her eyes.
When the doctor declared she was gone, Peter's father put a hand on his shoulder.
"No crying," he said firmly. "It accomplishes nothing."
Peter obeyed.
His tears retreated inward, becoming seeds of grief that would grow in silence.

The manor, once filled with warm light, now felt colder.
Quieter.
Harsher.
It would never be the same.

CHAPTER SIX
The House Learns Silence

After his mother's death, footsteps in the manor seemed softer, as if the house itself were mourning. Servants spoke in whispers. Curtains remained half-drawn. The warmth his mother had carried seemed to dissipate into the walls.

Peter's father returned to routine swiftly.

"Life continues," Raymond said. "We honour the dead by upholding discipline."

Peter wasn't sure that was true.

At school, teachers said he had changed, grown quieter, more serious, more contained. His classmates invited him to play, but Peter felt something inside him had closed. He had tasted loss and learned that affection came at a cost he was reluctant to pay again. He became the boy his father expected: well-mannered, focused, silent.

But not because he believed in the rules.

Because he feared breaking would make him weak.

CHAPTER SEVEN
Becoming a Whitfield

At fifteen, Peter began accompanying his father on
business trips. Trading firms. Warehouses.
Auction houses filled with relics from distant lands.
"Observe," Raymond said. "Absorb. This will all be
yours."
Peter watched men shake hands over deals that carried
fortunes.
He saw numbers dance across ledgers that frightened
him with their magnitude.
And he realised something.
His father did not wish him to inherit the business.
He wished him to become the business. To embody it.
Peter worked tirelessly.
Not out of ambition. Out of fear, fear of
disappointing a man who would never be satisfied.
But his heart remained somewhere else, tucked away
in memories of a mother who had taught him
softness.

Whitfield Manor grew heavier with age, or perhaps
Peter simply grew more aware of its burdens.
Raymond expected perfection. Expected obedience.
Expected his son to suppress every impulse that
wasn't aligned with the family legacy. But Peter
longed, secretly, tremblingly, for warmth.
For laughter.
For companionship.
He was twenty-four when his father informed him:
"You are to marry."
Peter blinked. "I beg your pardon?"

"I have negotiated terms. The Bennetts' daughter. Pretty enough. Clever. Comes from a respectable family. This alliance will strengthen our international ties. You will meet her on Tuesday."

"But I …"

"You will marry her, Peter. A Whitfield does not decline opportunity."

And Peter, as always, obeyed.

CHAPTER EIGHT
Present Day

Back in the cottage, Peter set down his mug as a tremor passed through him. Memories left him drained, as though each one tugged a thread tied deep inside.

Richard noticed.

"Do you need a minute?" he asked softly.

Peter breathed out slowly. "No."

"You sure?"

"Yes."

"Alright," Richard said, though his tone held doubt. He stood up to check the pill organiser on the shelf.

"Your medication's running low."

"I'll order more."

"I can do it…"

"I'll do it," Peter repeated.

Richard didn't argue further.

But his voice gentled.

"You know, Peter, people don't have to do everything alone."

Peter didn't answer.

He couldn't.

He looked toward the mantel, where the unopened charity letter waited.

The Dyslexia Development Trust.

His silent tribute to his lost son.

CHAPTER NINE
Rose Arrives - A Name That Echoed

Three mornings later, Peter waited for the familiar sound of cheerful knocking.
The kettle boiled. Two mugs waited on the counter, an arrangement he'd begun without admitting why.
At ten-thirty sharp, footsteps approached.
But the knock was softer.
When Peter opened the door, a young woman stood there with a clipboard pressed to her chest. Her dark hair was tied back neatly, and a gentle seriousness rested in her eyes.
"Good morning," she said. "I'm Rose. I'll be replacing Richard for a few weeks. He's unwell."
Peter's breath caught.
"Rose," he repeated.
"Yes," she smiled. "Rose Bennett."
The name. The face. The warmth.
Something shifted in the air.
And Peter had no idea yet how profoundly this young woman would change the rest of his life.

Peter stared at the young woman standing on his doorstep, the unexpected name rolling through him like a distant echo returning after decades underground.
Rose Bennett.
Her posture was formal at first, hands clasped lightly around her clipboard, as though bracing herself for resistance. She was used to older patients protesting new carers. She expected it.

But what she didn't expect was the way Peter's expression shifted, not merely startled, but deeply shaken, as if the universe had pulled a memory into the present and set it directly in front of him.

She softened her voice. "May I come in?"

Peter stepped aside automatically, still watching her as though she might disappear if he blinked.

The cottage felt smaller with her in it, not in an uncomfortable way, but in the way a quiet room feels fuller when sunlight spills into it. Rose moved gently, carefully, taking in the room as though reading its history. Her eyes rested briefly on the mantel, on the watch beneath its glass dome.

"It's a beautiful piece," she said quietly.

"It was my father's," Peter replied, his voice smaller than he intended.

Rose didn't push.

She simply nodded and placed her bag on the table.

"Richard left me some notes about your routine," she said. "But I prefer asking directly. Is there anything you'd like me to help with first?"

"I'm fine," Peter said.

She smiled. "Everyone says that."

"I mean it."

"I know. And yet I'm here."

Her tone wasn't confrontational.

It was understanding.

Peter sat in his chair, unsure what to do with his hands. He felt watched. Not judged - seen. It was unsettling.

"Would you like tea?" he asked after a moment.

Rose blinked, pleasantly surprised. "Yes, thank you."

Peter stood and moved to the kitchen. He hadn't made tea for anyone in years, not since …

He shook the thought away.

Rose took in the rest of the cottage. She noticed the quality of the furniture, the handmade craftsmanship of pieces too fine for such a modest home. She noticed the faint tension in the air … the ghost of someone who had once lived here, or the imprint of memories too heavy to leave.

When Peter returned with the tea, his hand trembled slightly as he handed her the mug.

"Thank you," she said warmly.

"You remind me of someone," Peter confessed before he could stop himself.

"Oh?" Rose asked, tilting her head.

"A person I knew a long time ago."

"Good memories, I hope."

He hesitated.

"Yes," he said. "And no."

Rose nodded as though she understood, and somehow, she did.

CHAPTER TEN
An Arrangement

———————————◆———————————

Years earlier - decades in the past, Peter found himself standing outside a refined townhouse in Kensington with a sense of resignation tightening his chest.

He had met Rose Bennett only once before the engagement was agreed. His father had arranged the meeting with the precision of a business transaction. What Peter expected was a polite stranger with a pleasing face.

What he found instead was a whirlwind.

Rose had been nineteen, bright, curious, and entirely uninterested in the cold formalities their fathers draped over the occasion.

"You look like you'd rather chew gravel than be here," she had whispered the moment their parents stepped out of hearing range.

Peter blinked, startled into honesty.

"I wouldn't go that far."

Her lips curved. "I would."

He didn't know what to say.

He had spent years cultivating silence.

She seemed allergic to it.

Rose glanced at him slyly. "Do you enjoy business dinners?"

"They're necessary."

"I didn't ask that."

He cleared his throat. "I suppose I tolerate them."

She laughed, not mockingly, but freely, as though they were already old friends.

That day left him unsettled. Rose was unpredictable, bold, filled with light. She challenged his instincts, cracked open spaces he had sealed years ago.
Their engagement was announced the next week.
Peter hadn't asked for it.
Rose hadn't either.
But she had shown up to the engagement dinner with a spark in her eye.
"If we're doomed to this arrangement," she whispered to him, "we may as well make something good of it."
Peter found he couldn't disagree.

CHAPTER ELEVEN
Wedding

It was Peter's wedding day; He's packed the book his father gave him. in a trunk the night before the wedding. He had hesitated, wondering if bringing it into married life would infect something pure. He took it anyway, out of habit, not devotion.

The church smelled of flowers and expectation. Guests filled the pews, the organ swelled, and Peter stood at the altar, stiff and unsure.

Then Rose entered.

Her veil framed a brightness that drew every gaze. She walked with confidence, as though she were stepping toward something she had chosen, rather than something chosen for her.

When she reached him, she whispered:

"You look like you're about to be audited."

"I feel like it," Peter murmured.

She laughed softly, and in that moment, his tension loosened.

Throughout the ceremony, Rose reached for his hand, just briefly, but enough to ground him. When they exchanged vows, her eyes were full of sincerity. She meant the words. Or at least, she intended to try.

Peter, for his part, had no idea how to love her the way she deserved.

But he wanted to learn.

After the wedding feast, Rose pulled him aside into the garden.

"I know you didn't choose this," she said gently. "But neither did I. Still... I think we could make something real. If we give it a chance."

Peter looked at her, truly looked, and felt something
inside shift.

"I'd like that," he said.

It was the most honest thing he had said in years.

CHAPTER TWELVE
Wife Who Brought Colour

Their home, a townhouse near the Thames, became warmer with Rose in it. She filled rooms with flowers, fresh linen, warm light. She opened windows even in winter "to let the house breathe," she said.
She spoke at breakfast.
She hummed while cooking.
She invited laughter without forcing it.
Peter found himself talking more.
Not much, but more than he ever had.
He told her about his mother.
About the manor.
About his father's expectations.
Rose listened with a soft sadness in her eyes.
"He taught you to fear emotion," she said one evening as they stood on the balcony overlooking the river.
"Yes."
"And you believed him."
"I didn't have a choice."
She reached for his hand.
"You do now."
Peter held her hand, stiff at first, then with gentle conviction.
He loved her.
He didn't know how to say it.
But she seemed to understand anyway.

CHAPTER THIRTEEN
The Daughter

Lily Rose Whitfield arrived on a bright spring morning, the kind of morning that made even the hospital windows glow. The world felt unusually still, as if it knew something important had taken its first breath.

Peter stood beside the bed, stiff and unsure, shifting his weight from one foot to the other. He had read about childbirth in clinical pamphlets, but nothing prepared him for the moment the nurse placed the tiny, swaddled bundle into Rose's waiting arms.

"She's beautiful," Rose whispered, the words trembling with wonder.

Peter leaned closer. The sight of the child startled him. "She is," he said, and for a moment his voice cracked in a way he hadn't heard since he was a boy.

Rose looked up at him with warm surprise. "You sound happy."

Peter hesitated. Feelings were things he usually pressed down, sorted, and stored away. But now, standing here, watching Rose cradle their daughter

"I am," he said quietly. And he realised it was true.

Rose lifted the baby toward him. "Hold her."

He froze. "Rose, I don't, I might do something wrong."

"You won't." She guided his hands, steady and sure, until Lily rested against his chest.

Peter stared at the tiny face, soft, new, impossibly small. Her eyelids fluttered like fragile wings. A faint sound escaped her lips, not quite a cry.

"She looks so… fragile," he murmured.

Rose smiled. "She's stronger than you think. Look."
Lily's little fingers curled around Peter's thumb with
surprising determination. Her grip was small, but
certain.
Something inside him softened, something he didn't
know he still had. It felt like a door he'd kept bolted
for years had shifted, even if only by an inch.
Rose watched him, her expression turning tender.
"She already knows you."
He swallowed, overwhelmed by the strange, aching
warmth spreading through him.
But then, like a cold draft, his father's voice slipped
through his thoughts.
Don't be sentimental.
Children are responsibilities, not indulgences.
Affection makes you weak.
The old lessons tightened around him. He could
almost feel the weight of the leather-bound family
book pressing down on his shoulders.
Peter looked at Lily again, her tiny fist wrapped
around his thumb, her breath soft against his shirt.
Something inside him rebelled.
He lowered his head and kissed her forehead.
It was a small gesture. A quiet one.
But it was defiance, pure and simple.
A promise he didn't yet know how to keep.
Rose reached for his hand. "She will bring out the best
in you, Peter."
He didn't answer. Not because he disagreed, but
because he hoped she was right, and that hope
frightened him more than anything.
For the first time in his life, he felt a love that wasn't
tied to expectation or duty.
It was simple.

Immediate.
Undeniable.

CHAPTER FOURTEEN
Pressure and distance

Years passed. Rose remained warm, patient, loving.
Lily grew into a clever, sharp-eyed child with her
mother's warmth and her father's stubbornness.
But Raymond Whitfield grew older, and demanding.
"You need a son," he insisted during a family dinner.
"A girl cannot carry the company legacy."
Rose looked at Peter, heart sinking.
"Your father doesn't decide our family," she
whispered later that night.
Peter wanted to believe that.
But decades of obedience were hard to unravel.
The doctor warned Rose against a second pregnancy.
"It could be dangerous," he said. "Her body took a
toll after the first."
Raymond dismissed this. "Nonsense. Women have
children all the time."
Peter hesitated, one moment of weakness that shifted
the course of four lives.
And Rose, wanting to please him, wanting harmony,
wanting to believe it would be alright…
became pregnant again.

CHAPTER FIFTEEN
Present Tensions

Back in the cottage, Rose noted the medication levels while Peter watched her with cautious fascination.

"You're very thorough," he observed.

"My mother taught me to do things properly."

"And she was a nurse?"

Rose paused, fingers stilling on the pill organiser.

"No," she said quietly. "She was… many things. Strong. Stubborn. Kind."

Peter sensed a heaviness in her tone.

"You miss her?"

"Yes."

The cottage fell into gentle silence.

Then Rose looked up with a small, sad smile.

"I think you would have liked her."

Something in Peter's chest tightened.

"I suppose we'll never know," he said softly.

Rose watched him then, properly, deeply, as if trying to read a story written behind his eyes.

"You look like someone who has missed a lot of people," she said gently.

Peter's throat constricted.

"I have," he whispered.

CHAPTER SIXTEEN
The Son and the Guilt

Rose's pregnancy was difficult, her colour faded, and her strength waned. She moved through the house like a candle burning too quickly.

The doctor visited frequently.

"You must rest," he insisted.

But Rose was restless because she was frightened, and because Peter hadn't found the courage to tell his father no.

One night, she clutched Peter's arm.

"What if something happens?"

Peter held her, just for a moment.

"I won't let anything happen."

She gave him a tired smile.

"You say that as if it's in your control."

Their son was born prematurely on a grey winter morning.

Weak.

Small.

Struggling.

Rose held him only briefly before she slipped into unconsciousness. She never woke again.

Peter's grief was a quiet explosion, a collapse he couldn't display. His father, standing beside him in the hospital hallway, said:

"You have a son. Focus on that."

Peter wanted to scream.

He didn't.

He took the baby boy home, a fragile ribbon connecting him to a wife he had loved more than he could express.

CHAPTER SEVENTEEN
The Hidden Letters

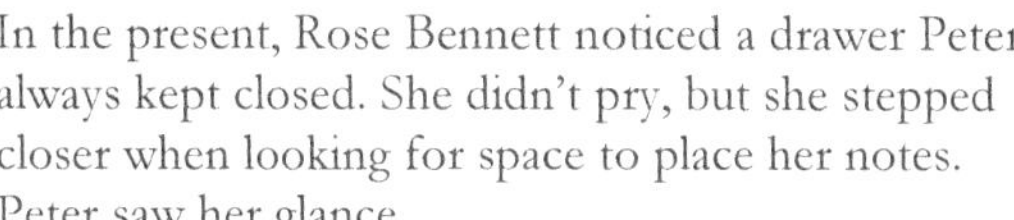

In the present, Rose Bennett noticed a drawer Peter always kept closed. She didn't pry, but she stepped closer when looking for space to place her notes.
Peter saw her glance.
"Those are old things," he said.
She nodded. "Everyone has those."
He opened the drawer himself, something he hadn't done in years.
Inside were:

- A stack of envelopes from dyslexia charities
- A small blue blanket
- A photograph of a boy with bright eyes
- And a bundle of letters addressed to *Lily*.

Peter closed the drawer before she could read further.
Rose didn't ask.
Some things needed time.
And time had begun to move differently in the little cottage.

CHAPTER EIGHTEEN
A Fragile Beginning

Thomas entered the world small and quiet, as if he were testing the air before trusting it. His cry, when it finally came, was thin and breathy. The nurses exchanged looks they tried to hide, but Peter caught them anyway. He forced himself to stay focused on the tiny bundle placed in his arms, on the warmth pressed against his chest, on the truth he was already trying desperately to accept.

Rose had seen her son for only a heartbeat before her eyes fluttered closed.

Her voice had been soft, barely more than breath.

He has your spirit.

Those were the last words she ever spoke.

The silence that followed her passing settled into Peter's bones. Yet when he held Thomas, a fragile comfort threaded through the grief. The boy curled his tiny fingers around Peter's shirt, and Peter stood there, motionless, afraid to breathe in case he broke something so delicate.

In the first years, Thomas clung to him with determined little hands. Peter often sat beside the crib until dawn, watching the gentle rise and fall of the small chest. Each breath soothed something raw inside him. For the first time in his life, he felt the instinct to protect without restraint, without calculation, without fear of appearing too soft.

But in quieter moments, the past slipped in.

The book his father had given him still sat on a high shelf in his study, the cracked spine turned inward so he wouldn't have to see it. He tried not to think of the

words written inside, yet they clung to him like dust
that had settled under his skin.

*Strength is built through silence. Emotion is an indulgence of the
weak.*

Years ago, he had accepted those lines as truth. Now,
as he watched his son sleep, he realised how wrong
they were, and how tightly they had shaped him.

Looking at Thomas, he felt the words grind against
the instincts rising in him.

For the first time, he let himself ignore them.

Thomas grew slowly, always trailing slightly behind
other children in size and speech, but he radiated a
gentle warmth that drew people in. He laughed easily,
trusted without hesitation, and leaned into affection
the way flowers lean toward the sun.

Tutors came and went, each puzzled by the same
thing. He mixed up letters, reversed words, and forgot
numbers the moment they left the page. A specialist
visited when Thomas was five. She sat with Peter in
the parlour, her voice kind.

"I believe he's dyslexic," she said. "He understands
everything. He just learns differently. He'll need
patience and structure."

Peter nodded. He had prepared himself for something
worse. This, he believed, they could manage.

But Raymond saw only a flaw.

"This child must take over the firm one day," he said,
his tone clipped, his eyes hard. "How can he lead if he
cannot even read?"

"He is five," Peter said calmly.

"Children become their weaknesses if we let them.
Correct it early."

Peter swallowed the anger rising in his chest. He said
nothing more, but later that night, when the house

had gone still, he climbed the stairs to his study. He reached for the old book and opened it to the page his father had once tapped with cold conviction.

The sentence stared up at him from the yellowed paper.

Emotion is an indulgence of the weak.

Peter closed the book slowly. For a long moment, he simply held it, thumb brushing the brittle edge of the page. Then he shut it with a soft snap and returned it to the shelf.

For the first time, he wished he had burned it years ago.

Lily adored Thomas from the moment the newborn was placed in her lap. She read to him in animated voices, shielding him from the world's sharp edges. She brushed his hair from his forehead the way Rose once brushed hers. In every way that mattered, she stepped into the space her mother had left behind.

But with every act of devotion toward her brother, the distance between Lily and Peter grew wider. Whatever grief she carried, she carried pointedly.

One evening, when Thomas was six and she was a teenager who had long outgrown her mother's softness, she spoke quietly as Peter stood by the hallway door.

"You should be here more," she said, her voice steady but full of accusation.

Peter straightened. "I do what I can."

"You say that every time. And it never changes."

The words hit him in the place he tried hardest to protect, the place where guilt had carved its home.

He opened his mouth, ready to defend himself, ready to say *I'm trying,* but the words stuck. Silence filled the space instead, heavy and familiar.

Lily walked away without waiting for an answer. Thomas called after her from the sitting room, and she turned back with a smile meant only for him. Peter stood alone in the corridor, the echo of her words lingering long after she had gone.

CHAPTER NINETEEN
Winter Illness

The illness began with a soft, nagging cough that clung to the edges of Thomas's sleep. Within days, the sound deepened into something harsher, each breath rattling through his small chest. The doctor visited more than once, his concern growing each time.

"He needs constant attention," he said quietly. "Possibly hospital care."

Before Peter could speak, Raymond shut the idea down.

"Doctors always dramatize. It is a cold. The meeting in Geneva is vital. The firm cannot afford disruption."

Peter hesitated. He looked at Thomas's pale face, then at the documents spread across his desk. Years of obedience, years of being shaped by another man's opinions, clouded his judgment just when clarity mattered most.

He knelt beside Thomas's bed. "I will be gone only two days," he said, keeping his voice even. "I will be back by the weekend."

Thomas nodded, exhausted. "Okay, Daddy."

Lily stood in the doorway, her arms crossed tightly, her eyes fierce with the kind of anger that comes from fear.

"You are leaving again," she said.

"The meeting is important."

"So is he."

"I know."

"You do not behave like you know."

He reached out for her shoulder, but she stepped back before his hand touched her.

The flight was delayed.
Storms closed airports.
The meeting stretched longer than expected.
Two days slipped into three.
By the time Peter returned home, dread had already
settled into his bones.

CHAPTER TWENTY
The Last Breath

———————— ✦ ————————

The house was silent when he entered. Not simply quiet, but unnervingly still, as though it had sealed itself against the truth waiting inside.

A nurse met him halfway up the stairs. Her expression told him everything before she spoke.

"I am very sorry, Mr Whitfield. He worsened yesterday. We did everything we could."

Peter climbed the stairs slowly, each step heavy, each breath harder to take. When he reached the nursery, Thomas lay motionless beneath the blanket he loved. His small face looked peaceful in a way that made the sight even more unbearable.

Peter knelt beside the bed and covered his face with his hands. No tears came, only the deep internal tearing of someone who had spent a lifetime holding back emotion. Grief, denied for years, had nowhere to go. It simply pressed inward, suffocating in its weight.

Lily stood behind him. When she spoke, her voice was soft but shaped by heartbreak.

"You left," she said. "You left just like you left Mum."

"Lily, please listen to me."

"He needed you."

"I know."

"You did not come."

"I tried."

"You always try," she whispered. "Trying is not enough."

He reached for her, but she stepped away so quickly it felt like rejection in its purest form.

"You love work more than any of us," she said. "Now Thomas is gone because you weren't here."

The words pierced him in the one place he had never learned to protect.

She went to her room, grabbed a small bag, and ran downstairs. Peter followed, desperate, stumbling more than walking.

"Lily, do not go," he said. "I am begging you."

She paused at the open door, her back still turned.

"I cannot live in this house anymore. Not with you."

Then she left.

The sound of the door closing echoed for years afterward.

CHAPTER TWENTY-ONE
The Hollow Years

The weeks that followed blurred into a heavy fog. The manor, once filled with voices and footsteps and warmth, now felt cavernous and cold. Every room held an absence Peter could not escape. The silence of three lost lives grew louder with each passing day.

One evening, he opened the drawer in his study and found the book his father had given him. The cracked leather cover stared up at him like an accusation. He opened it to the familiar page and reread the line that had shaped so much of his life.

Emotion is an indulgence of the weak.

He closed the book slowly, pressing his palm over the worn cover. He wished he had never allowed those words to guide him. The book should have been thrown into the fire, but a part of him held on to it, as though discarding it meant admitting everything he had done wrong.

That winter, Raymond suffered a stroke and died several months later. Peter felt no triumph, no closure, only a strange emptiness. The man who had built the structure of his life and broken so much of it was gone.

Peter sold the manor first. Then the townhouse. Then the smaller estate. His world shrank until it fit inside a modest cottage, a place without echoes or expectations. A place where the book lived in a drawer he rarely opened, hidden yet always near enough to remind him of the life he had failed to protect.

He stepped away from the firm quietly, without ceremony.

He began donating large sums to dyslexia charities in Thomas's name. He requested anonymity, and the organisations honoured it. Each thank-you letter was tucked into the same drawer as the old book, the two sets of papers lying together like conflicting chapters of the same life.

Years passed. He lived alone.

Sometimes it felt like punishment.

Sometimes it felt like the only way he knew how to survive.

CHAPTER TWENTY-TWO
The Visitor Who Stayed

When Rose Bennett entered his life, something long dormant stirred in Peter, as if a small draft had slipped into a room he kept sealed for years. She carried herself with quiet confidence, her steps unhurried, her voice calm, her presence never demanding more space than he allowed.

She moved through the cottage with gentle respect, always asking before she touched a drawer or straightened a cushion. She didn't rush conversation, nor did she fill silence with unnecessary words. Instead, she made the silence feel different, less like an accusation and more like a place where someone could rest.

One afternoon, she watched him lower himself into the armchair, her eyes thoughtful.

"You did not sleep well," she said.

"No," he admitted.

"Nightmares or memories?"

"Memories."

Rose nodded slowly, as though the answer was familiar to her. "My mother used to say that memories are like locked rooms. You do not heal by standing outside them. You heal by opening the door and looking around."

Peter lifted his gaze to hers. Something in those words struck a deep, tender place inside him.

"I have avoided many rooms," he said quietly.

"You are opening them now," she replied. "Even if you do not realise it."

She turned back to sort the medication box, her hands steady, movements unhurried.

Peter watched her, sensing again that strange, unsettling familiarity he couldn't quite name. It was in the way she tilted her head when she listened, or the small pause before she smiled. Tiny echoes of someone he once loved fiercely and lost too soon.

The next time she smiled, something tugged deep within him, a faint, painful, comforting pull. The curve of her lips, the softness in her eyes, the gentle patience in her posture. For a moment, he saw Rose, his wife. Not in her features, but in her warmth.

And somewhere in the cottage, in the quiet drawer where he kept the old book with its harsh lessons, it lay as still as ever.

Waiting.

Watching.

Knowing that the truth, at last, was beginning to take shape.

CHAPTER TWENTY-THREE
The Echo of a Name

A week after Rose Bennett began visiting the cottage, Peter found himself watching her more closely than he intended. It wasn't suspicion. It wasn't discomfort. It was something else, something unsettling and strangely familiar.

It was in the way she listened, quiet and attentive.

The way she tilted her head slightly, as if making space in her mind for every word.

The gentleness in her hands.

The careful smile she offered when she thought he wasn't looking.

They were small things, but they stirred memories he thought he had buried for good.

That morning began as simply as any other. Rose moved through the kitchen, checking his medication and making small adjustments to the pill organiser. Peter filled the kettle and waited for it to boil. She spoke about the day's weather, about the flowers she had seen blooming along the lane, about the small things that made mornings feel softer.

Peter listened, but underneath her voice something tugged at him, a feeling just out of reach, like a word on the tip of the tongue.

Finally, unable to quiet the unease, he said, "May I ask you something?"

Rose looked up immediately. "Of course."

He hesitated before choosing the simplest question. "How old are you?"

"I turned twenty-eight in April," she said.

The answer did nothing to calm him. If anything, the pressure beneath his ribs tightened, as though something inside him recognised a truth his mind had not yet caught up with.

He tried again, slower this time.

"And your mother… what was her name?"

The pause before Rose answered was small, but not empty. Her expression changed, touched by a grief that had clearly settled long ago.

"Her name was Lily," she said quietly.

Peter's fingers loosened.

The cup slipped from his hand, striking the tiles and shattering at his feet.

Rose startled at the sound. "Peter? Are you hurt?"

But he barely heard her.

He felt as if the room had tilted, as though decades had collapsed into this single moment. Rose hurried toward him and placed a steadying hand on his arm. "Sit," she said softly. "Before you fall."

He let her guide him to the chair. The world around him blurred at the edges, but that one word repeated in his mind like a tolling bell.

"Lily," he whispered.

His daughter's name.

Rose nodded slowly. "Yes. Lily Rose Bennett. My mother."

The air in the cottage shifted.

A door long shut inside Peter seemed to finally open. And in the quiet that followed, he felt something break, not in pain, but in recognition.

A truth he had never expected to face had found him at last.

CHAPTER TWENTY-FOUR
The Weight of Unsaid Things

Rose brought him a glass of water and sat across from him. She didn't rush him. She didn't push for answers. She simply waited, steady and patient, giving him room to breathe.

Peter's voice trembled when he finally spoke.

"Your mother… where did she grow up?"

Rose folded her hands in her lap, thinking back.

"In the countryside near Bath. She never said much about her childhood. Most of what I know came in fragments."

"What kind of fragments?"

"She said her family was complicated. That she left home when she was young. She never explained why." Rose lowered her gaze. "I think the memories hurt too much to speak about."

Peter felt the room shift. A slow, heavy tilt he couldn't steady.

"She never mentioned her father?" he asked quietly. Rose shook her head.

"Not often. And when she did, she changed the subject quickly. When I was little, I thought she was angry with him. As I grew older, I realised she was sad. She kept a box of letters she never opened. They were addressed to her in handwriting I didn't recognise."

Peter closed his eyes. The truth landed with a weight that hollowed him.

"Oh God," he whispered. "Those letters were from me."

Rose lifted her head, surprise softening her features. "You wrote to her?"

"For years," he said. "Every birthday. Every Christmas. And in between. I begged her to come home. Or at least tell me she was alive." His voice cracked on the last word. "I didn't know if she ever read them."

Rose's breath caught.

"She kept them with her. Every time we moved. She never threw them away."

Peter pressed a shaking hand to his forehead. The revelation struck like a blow, but one wrapped in unexpected tenderness. He didn't know whether to grieve or be grateful.

"And you?" he asked softly. "Why did you come here?"

Rose hesitated, gathering herself.

"My mother became ill last year. Cancer. She fought as long as she could, but near the end… she knew."

Peter's heart clenched.

"One night, she told me the truth," Rose continued.

"What truth?" he whispered.

"She said she had run from someone she loved once but couldn't bear to face again. That her anger had turned into regret, then into longing she didn't know how to speak aloud." Rose's voice softened. "Then she told me his name. She told me your name."

Peter gripped the edge of the table, his knuckles white.

Rose continued quietly.

"she said you were the only family I had left. And she asked me to find you."

Peter bowed his head.

The grief that rose in him was gentle, almost reverent. A grief shaped by love instead of loss.

He placed his hand over his eyes.
"Your mother was my daughter," he whispered.
"My Lily."
Rose nodded slowly.
"I know."

CHAPTER TWENTY- FIVE
The Breaking and the Holding

Peter felt the air thicken until it was hard to breathe. He tried to rise from the chair, but Rose laid a steady hand on his arm.

"Wait. You are shaking."

"I do not understand," he whispered. His fingers clenched around the wooden arms of the chair. "How can you be here? After everything I did… after everything I failed to do."

Rose knelt beside him so he would not have to look down in shame.

Her voice was quiet, steady.

"You did not fail her completely."

Peter's head shook, a small, broken movement.

"I drove her away. I wasn't there when she needed me most. I became the man I swore I would never become."

"You did make mistakes," Rose said, not sparing him the truth. "Serious ones. Ones that hurt her deeply." She softened then. "But you tried. You reached for her the only way you knew how. You wrote. You waited. You hoped. You never stopped loving her."

Peter's breath trembled.

Rose continued gently.

"And she never hated you. She missed you in ways she could barely speak about. She carried that longing her entire life."

Peter covered his face with both hands.

For decades, tears had been denied, pushed down, taught out of him like a bad habit. But now they came freely, unstoppable, falling through his fingers as though some long-locked reservoir had finally broken open. The sound wasn't loud. It was quiet, soft, and steady. The kind of crying that heals without asking permission.

Rose placed her hand on his arm, grounding him.

"I think she wanted us to find each other," she said softly. "So, neither of us would be alone anymore."

Peter lowered his hands slowly. His eyes were red, but clear in a way she had not seen before. He looked at her as though seeing her not just as a visitor, but as the bridge between everything he had lost and everything, he still had left.

"Rose," he said, voice trembling. "I never imagined I would be allowed this. To know you. To know even a small part of her again."

Rose's expression warmed.

"You are my grandfather," she said. "That does not change because life was hard. Or because mistakes were made."

Something inside him loosened, like a knot finally giving way. He let out a long breath that felt like it had been trapped inside him for years.

"I want to be," he said. And he meant it with every part of him that still knew how to love.

CHAPTER TWENTY-SIX
The Drawer That Always Stayed Closed

Later that afternoon, when his strength returned and his breathing steadied, Peter reached for the drawer he had avoided for years. His hand hovered over the handle for a long moment, as though he were touching the edge of an old wound.

Then he pulled it open.

Inside lay the fragments of a life he had never known how to face:

The old leather-bound book his father once pressed into his hands, its corners worn and softened by time.

A stack of unopened letters from dyslexia charities, each one a quiet echo of the son he lost.

Thomas's small blue blanket, still carrying the faint shape of a child long gone.

A faded photograph of Lily at age ten, eyes bright with a spark that had terrified him and moved him in equal measure.

And several envelopes marked Return to sender.

Rose sat beside him in silence, her presence gentle, her stillness respectful. There was no rush, no pressure. Just the shared weight of things finally being witnessed.

Peter touched the book first, brushing a thumb over the cracked spine.

"This was my father's legacy," he said. "A legacy that cost me nearly everything."

Rose studied the book, then looked at him.

"Why did you keep it?"

He hesitated before answering.

"I could not throw it away," he said quietly. "Not

because I believed in it. But because it was the only thing he ever gave me with his own hands."

Rose nodded, seeing more in his words than he had meant to reveal.

Pain. Loyalty. Loneliness.

And the deep hunger for approval that had shaped so much of his life.

She lifted the photograph of Lily and traced its edges with gentle fingers.

"She looked like my mum," she whispered.

Peter leaned closer. His breath caught at the sight of that familiar smile.

"Yes," he said softly. "Exactly like her. Fierce. Brilliant. So full of life."

Rose placed the photograph back in the drawer but kept her hand resting on Peter's arm, grounding him.

"Will you tell me about her?" she asked.

"Who she was before everything fell apart? I want to know her the way you knew her."

Peter closed his eyes for a moment, steadying himself. When he opened them again, the grief was still there, but so was something else. Something lighter.

The beginning of release.

"Yes," he said. "I owe her that much. And I owe you the truth."

The drawer stayed open.

For the first time in decades, the past did not press down on him until he could not breathe.

It did not accuse.

It did not shame.

Instead, it waited.

Patient.

Quiet.

Inviting him to speak.

CHAPTER TWENTY-SEVEN
A Father Learns to Speak

The afternoon settled gently over the cottage, warm light falling through the windows in soft stripes that stretched across the floorboards. Dust floated lazily in the glow, turning the quiet moment into something almost sacred. The open drawer between Peter and Rose felt like a doorway to a room he had kept locked for far too long.

Rose rested her hand on the photograph of Lily.

"You said you would tell me about her," she whispered.

Peter nodded, feeling something loosen inside him. A part of his heart he thought was permanently shut now stood ajar, and the air behind it was warm with memory.

"She was born on a spring morning," he began. "The whole house changed that day. Even my father pretended to be pleased, though he tried to hide it. She cried loudly the moment she arrived. I remember thinking she had more spirit in her first breath than I had in my entire childhood."

Rose's lips curved into a knowing smile.

"She always said she was impossible as a baby."

Peter laughed softly, a sound rough from disuse.

"She was impossible in the brightest way. Climbing everything, exploring every corner, touching things she should not touch. Her laugh filled the house. When she was three, she'd run down the breakfast corridor with her arms stretched out like wings, shouting that she was a bird and needed to fly. The servants adored her."

Rose looked at him over the photograph.

"And you?"

He paused, choosing honesty over habit.

"I adored her too. I just… did not know how to show it."

Rose didn't soften the truth.

"She felt that. Even when she told me she loved you, she felt it."

"I know," Peter whispered. His eyes drifted to the window as though expecting to see the past strolling across the garden. "Every time I tried to show her affection, the words caught in my throat. It was as if my father was standing behind me, watching, waiting for me to fail."

Rose tilted her head, studying him with quiet empathy. "Mum used to say she always believed you loved her. She just wished she didn't have to guess."

Peter's voice lowered to a fragile whisper.

"I wish I had known how to give her certainty."

CHAPTER TWENTY-EIGHT
Stories That Bloom in the Silence

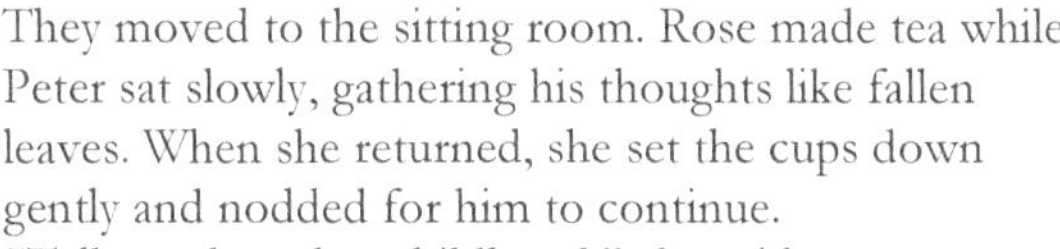

They moved to the sitting room. Rose made tea while Peter sat slowly, gathering his thoughts like fallen leaves. When she returned, she set the cups down gently and nodded for him to continue.

"Tell me about her childhood," she said.

Peter's expression softened.

"She loved the garden more than any other place. It was her sanctuary. When she was six, she planted a row of tulips. They were crooked, uneven, scattered in places they shouldn't have been. But she adored them. She watered them twice a day. When they finally bloomed, she ran inside shouting for me to come and see them. I still remember her hair catching the sunlight when she pulled me outside. She was… pure light."

Rose blinked hard, her eyes glistening.

"She still loved tulips. Every spring she bought a bunch and put them on the windowsill."

Peter felt a warmth move through him.

"I am glad she carried that with her."

There was a pause before Rose asked, "What was she like with Thomas?"

Peter's breath tightened.

"She was his second mother. Steady when I couldn't be. Patient when I didn't understand him. She sat with him for hours, teaching him letters, drawing shapes, singing songs. He trusted her more than anyone in the world."

Rose nodded slowly.

"She was like that with me too. She could calm storms without raising her voice."

Peter looked at her with something close to awe.

"You have her way with people. It is like seeing her reflection move through the world again."

Rose lowered her gaze, touched but quiet.

The room felt full then, full of Lily's laughter, her presence, her stubborn fire, woven between their voices, blooming in the silence they now shared.

CHAPTER TWENTY-NINE
What Lily Never Said

After a long stillness, Rose spoke again.

"Mum never told me much about the night she left. She only said she was hurting. That there were things she wished she could forget. But she never gave details. Was there something she couldn't face?"

Peter closed his eyes, bracing himself.

"Yes," he whispered. "She blamed me for Thomas's death. And she had every right to."

Rose waited, letting him find the words in his own time.

"I left him," Peter said. "I told myself it was work. Duty. Responsibility. But the truth was simpler. I was afraid. I did not know how to say no to my father. I didn't know how to choose my own child over his commands."

His voice cracked.

"I thought I had time. I thought Thomas would recover."

He swallowed hard.

"And I was wrong."

Rose touched his hand lightly, her gesture gentle and steady.

"You were human," she said quietly.

"I was cowardly," Peter replied. "And Lily saw it clearly. She said the words I deserved to hear. When she left, I let her go because I was too ashamed to stop her. I tried later, again and again, but she had built a wall I could not cross."

"She was stubborn," Rose murmured. "So am I."

For the first time since the conversation began, Peter managed a fragile smile.

"You have her fire."

Rose returned the smile softly.

"And your quiet."

Peter exhaled, the breath trembling on its way out.

"Perhaps between us," she said, "we can rebuild something she would be proud of."

Peter nodded, a slow, hopeful movement.

"I hope so," he whispered. And for the first time in years, he meant it.

CHAPTER THIRTY
The Garden That Waited

In the days that followed, Rose brought warmth to every corner of the cottage. She moved easily between caring for Peter and listening to his stories, each one another thread sewn into the tapestry of Lily's memory.

One afternoon she asked, "Is there a garden here?"

Peter hesitated.

"Yes, but I have not tended it in years."

"Let us see it."

He resisted at first, but something in her tone made refusal impossible.

They stepped outside, walking along the stone path behind the cottage. The garden had once been beautiful, full of wild colour and quiet corners. Now the beds were overgrown, the soil dry, the vines collapsed beneath their own weight. Rose knelt at one of the beds, brushing aside brittle leaves.

"There is life here," she said. "It only needs care."

Peter felt something stir in him.

"I am not sure I know how to begin."

"Then let me help you," Rose said simply.

She dug her fingers into the soil.

Peter watched her hands, so much like Lily's, so much like Rose's mother's hands must have been.

"Gardens forgive," she said. "They do not remember neglect forever."

The words lodged deep inside him.

CHAPTER THIRTY-ONE
The Letter She Brought with Her

The evening had a softness to it. Outside, the sky was turning a muted blue, and the first stars were beginning to appear. Inside the cottage, a lamp cast a warm circle of light over the sitting room. It was within that circle that Rose sat, her hands lightly resting on something folded in her lap.

Peter noticed the way she kept touching it, as though steadying herself.

"You have something on your mind," he said quietly.

She looked up, then down again at the papers she held.

"I do. And I have been trying to find the right moment."

Peter waited. He had learned, at last, that some truths took time to surface and that pushing only frightened them back into silence.

Rose took a breath.

"When my mother died," she began, "she left me a small box. I did not open it straight away. It took me weeks before I could bear it."

Peter's hands tightened slightly on the arms of his chair.

"In that box," Rose continued, "was a letter. For you."

He stared at her, the words not quite forming meaning.

"For me?"

"Yes. She wrote it over many years. She started it when she was a child, added to it when she was older, and finished it as an adult. She never sent it. She kept it. And before she died, she told me to give it to you when I found you."

She placed the folded pages gently on the table between them, as if setting something fragile in a place of honour.

"I have read it," she said. "More than once. I think you have a right to read it now."

The room grew very still.

Peter looked at the pages. His hands did not move at first. Then, slowly, he reached out and drew them toward him.

His voice was almost a whisper.

"Will you stay while I read it?"

Rose nodded.

"I will."

He unfolded the letter. The top part was written in large, looping handwriting, the letters uneven, the lines tilted. The writing of a child.

Peter steadied himself and began to read.

CHAPTER THIRTY-TWO
Lily Rose as a Child

The first words on the page were simple.
Papa,
I found Mummy's letter today. I know I should not have opened
the box, but I missed her. She said you love me even if you do
not say it. I think she is right. Because sometimes I see you look
at me like you want to tell me something kind and then you
don't. But your eyes look soft. I like when they look soft.

Peter lowered the page, his breath catching.
Rose moved her chair closer without speaking,
offering comfort without intrusion.

He lifted the letter again.
Sometimes I cry in the garden because I know you don't like
when I cry. But I think you hear me. I think you check the
window because I hear the floor creak. If that is you, thank you
for checking.
Love,
Lily

Peter's voice broke.
"I always checked," he whispered. "I thought she
never noticed."
Rose touched his arm gently.
"She saw everything."
Peter closed his eyes, steadying himself.
When he opened them again, he saw that her
handwriting changed on the next page. More
controlled. Still emotional, but older.

"She kept writing," he murmured.
Rose nodded. "She always meant to send it someday."

CHAPTER THIRTY-THREE
The Anger That Hid Her Love

Peter continued reading.

Papa,
I hate you. I hate that you told me not to cry at the hospital
when Thomas was sick. I hated that you stayed silent when I
was scared. I hated that you looked angry when I think you
were really frightened.

Peter flinched.

But even when I hated you, there were things I remembered:
The night you sat alone after Mummy died. I heard you crying.
I never told you.
The red shoes you bought me even though you pretended you
didn't hear me asking for them.
The tea you left outside my door on the mornings I couldn't get
out of bed.
The birthday you let me eat two slices of cake and let
Grandfather shout at you instead of me.
I remembered all of it.
I still do.
Lily

Peter's breath shook as he lowered the letter.
Rose spoke softly.
"She kept every small thing you did. Even when she
was hurting."
He nodded, wiping his face with the back of his hand.
"And there is one more section," Rose said quietly.
"Written when she was grown. When I was little."

Peter braced himself.
Then he read on.

CHAPTER THIRTY-FOUR
The Forgiveness She Carried

Papa,

I am writing this last part now because I'm older, and I understand things I never did as a child.

When I held my daughter for the first time, I finally understood what fear feels like when you love someone too much. How love can twist into silence. How worry can turn into distance. How easily fear can be mistaken for coldness.

I understood you.

I thought of you standing in doorways, not knowing how to come in. I thought of every time you chose Grandfather over me and how much that must have cost you. I thought of how young you were when he taught you the wrong kind of strength.

I forgive you.

I forgave you when I knew what it was to be a parent. I forgave you when I watched my daughter sleep and felt terrified, she might disappear. I forgave you when I understood how love can break you open.

I want you to know this clearly:

I loved you even when I was angry.

I loved you when I left.

I loved you when I pretended I didn't.

I loved you in every version of my life.

Your Lily

Peter let the pages fall gently onto his lap. His shoulders trembled. Not with the old, silent grief he had known his entire life, but with something fuller, heavier, alive.

Rose placed her hand over his, anchoring him.

"Take your time," she whispered.

CHAPTER THIRTY-FIVE
Her Presence in the Room

When Peter finally folded the letter, he did so with a tenderness he had never used with anything his father had given him.

"She didn't die hating me," he whispered.

The wonder in his voice was almost childlike.

Rose shook her head.

"She carried you with her. Even when she struggled to admit it. Even when she was angry. She talked about you more than she realised."

Peter looked at her, startled.

"She did?"

"Little things," Rose said. "How you walked on the outside of the pavement. How you checked the windows twice. How your tea was too strong. She remembered everything. She just didn't know how to say it without reopening old wounds."

Peter pressed the folded letter to his chest.

"I wasted so many years."

"You did," Rose said honestly.

"But you do not have to waste the years you have left."

He looked toward the window, toward the garden waiting outside.

For the first time since childhood, he wanted to step toward hope.

CHAPTER THIRTY-SIX
The Book Finds the Light

That evening, while Rose prepared supper, Peter returned to the drawer he had avoided for most of his life. He slid it open slowly, as though disturbing something asleep. For decades he had used it only to hide things he could not bear to confront. But now, with the letter still warm in his pocket, something in him had shifted.

This time, he reached not for the memories tucked inside, but for the book that had shaped too much of him.

The old leather-bound volume.

Raymond's book.

His inheritance of silence.

The cracked spine creaked as he lifted it from the drawer.

Rose entered the room just as he set it gently on the table. She paused when she saw it.

"You chose to take it out," she said softly.

Peter nodded.

"I think it is time."

She sat across from him, not crowding him, but not letting him face this alone.

Peter opened the book to the familiar page. The line stared up at him, the one his father had tapped years ago.

Strength is built through silence. Emotion is an indulgence of the weak.

He used to think the sentence was carved into him like a rule etched onto stone.

Now it looked small.

Almost fearful.

"I lived by these words," he said. "I thought they would make me unbreakable."

Rose watched him carefully.

"They did not make you unbreakable," she said. "They made you isolated."

Peter let out a slow breath, one that carried years of weight.

"Yes," he said. "They did."

He turned the page.

Cold instructions.

Rigid rules.

Trade routes and ledger formats.

Advice that seemed less like guidance and more like chains.

"This book taught me how to be a Whitfield," he murmured. "But not how to be… anything else. Not how to be present. Or gentle. Or brave in the right way."

Rose folded her hands in her lap.

"Then let it teach you one last thing."

He looked at her.

"That you can choose to set it down," she said.

Peter stared at the cover.

Thin, cracked, tired.

A book built from fear masquerading as strength.

"I do not hate it," he said quietly. "I don't even know if I blame it. My father gave me what he had. It was not much, but it was his offering."

He brushed a hand along the worn leather.

"For years, I believed letting go meant dishonouring him," he said. "But now I know… holding onto this has only dishonoured my daughter. And myself."

He closed the book.
The click of the cover was soft, almost kind.
Rose smiled gently.
"Some endings don't need fire. Sometimes they need only honesty."
Peter placed the book aside, not with anger, not with bitterness, but with the quiet finality of someone laying a burden down.
It was the first time the book sat on the table without controlling anything inside him.
For the first time, it was only a book.

CHAPTER THIRTY-SEVEN
The First True Smile

Rose arrived early the next morning to find Peter already standing in the garden. The air was fresh and cool, the sky a soft wash of dawn. Peter stood by the patch they had cleared the day before, a small packet of tulip bulbs in his hands.

"I could not sleep," he said. "My mind kept returning to this place. To her. To all of them."

Rose stepped beside him, warmth settling between them like quiet sunlight.

"So you came out early?"

"No," he said, turning toward her. "I waited. I wanted to plant them with you."

She smiled gently. "Then let us begin."

They knelt beside each other in the soil. Rose tipped the bulbs into her palm, smooth, pale, full of hidden life, and handed one to Peter.

His hands trembled as he pressed the first bulb into the earth. Rose steadied him with a hand on his back, a gesture so simple it undid something in him.

They worked slowly, setting each bulb in a soft bed of earth. They did not measure or calculate. The row formed the way memory forms, uneven, honest, rooted in love rather than precision.

When they finished, Peter brushed soil from his palms and looked at the bed.

"She would have liked this," he said softly.

Rose nodded. "She would have loved it."

Peter turned to her with a softness she had never seen. "For the first time in many years," he said, "I feel something that resembles hope."

"And you deserve hope," Rose replied.
His mouth curved into a small smile, hesitant, fragile, but real.
It was the first true smile he had shown in decades.

CHAPTER THIRTY-EIGHT
The Attic That Waited

Later that afternoon, Rose suggested cleaning the small attic above the cottage. Peter hesitated only for a moment. Something in him had changed since reading Lily's words. The past no longer felt like a threat. It felt like a place he could finally walk through without losing himself.

They climbed the narrow stairs together. Dust swirled like pale glitter in the slanting light. The air smelled of old paper and forgotten summers.

Rose pointed toward a small wooden chest tucked in the corner beneath a blanket.

"What is that one?" she asked.

Peter frowned.

"I'm not sure. I haven't opened it since I moved in."

They carried it carefully downstairs and set it on the rug in the sitting room. When Peter lifted the lid, the first thing he saw was an embroidered handkerchief stitched with a single blue initial.

R.

Rose leaned closer.

"Your wife?"

"Yes," Peter said softly. "She embroidered that when she was expecting Lily."

Beneath it lay baby socks she had knitted, tiny and perfect. A faint smile touched Peter's face.

"She made these during long nights," he said. "She was always making something for someone she loved."

Rose's smile was gentle.

"She sounds like she had a soft heart."

"She did," Peter whispered. "Softer than anyone I know."

They sifted through the chest: a seashell Lily had collected, Thomas's wooden bird toy, a photograph of the four of them at the seaside, Peter younger, his wife glowing with joy, Lily laughing on his shoulders, Thomas curled in his mother's arms.

Then, near the bottom, Peter's hand stilled.

A bundle of letters, tied carefully with ribbon, rested beneath a folded shawl. The ribbon had faded to a washed-out red.

Rose's breath caught.

"These are from her?"

Peter lifted them with trembling hands.

"Yes," he said. "These are my wife's letters."

He sat back slowly, as though the room had tilted.

"She wrote to me," he whispered. "And I never knew."

CHAPTER THIRTY-NINE
The Letters Rose Left Behind

———————— ✦ ————————

Peter untied the ribbon with fingers that shook more from emotion than age. Rose sat beside him, close but silent, giving him the space to lead.

The first envelope had his name on it, written in the familiar curl of her handwriting.

He unfolded the letter.

My Peter,

I am writing this because I know you will never say what you feel, and I love you too much to leave the truth unspoken forever.

His breath caught. The room went quiet.

He read on.

You carry the world as if someone ordered you to hold it alone. You love quietly. You love without saying it. I see every effort, every small kindness you think goes unnoticed.

He paused, his eyes wet.

Rose touched his arm, grounding him.

He continued.

I worry about you. Not because you are weak, but because you refuse to let yourself be human. One day, when our children are grown, I hope you learn to put your father's voice down. I hope you learn to speak in your own.

Peter folded the letter against his chest.

"I never heard her say these things," he whispered.

"She wrote them for you," Rose said softly. "She trusted you would find them someday."

The next letter was dated several years later.

Peter,

I know you love the children. You show it in ways they don't always understand, but I do. When Lily cries, you stand outside her door pretending to tidy papers until she calms. When she is

frightened, you wait beside the stairs, so she sees your shape before she sees the darkness. She may not know, but I know.
Tears fell freely now.
Rose laid a hand on his back as he read the final letter.
If these pages ever reach your hands, it means time has passed and perhaps you are finally ready to hear me.
I want you to know that you were loved deeply. Imperfectly. Fiercely.
By me.
By our children.
And I pray that one day you will forgive yourself enough to love someone again.
Peter lowered the page, his entire body trembling.
His wife's voice felt alive again. Her warmth filled the spaces Lily's letter had already opened.
Rose wiped her eyes quietly.
"She wrote with so much tenderness. She must have loved you in every part of her life."
Peter nodded, barely breathing.
"And I never knew," he whispered.
"You do now," Rose said.

CHAPTER FORTY
Old Letters, New Understanding

They spent the next hours reading through letters, some short, some pages long. Memories folded between the ink. A life he once had, now returned to him in her own handwriting.

When the last letter was placed gently on the table, Peter leaned back and closed his eyes. He felt filled and emptied all at once.

"She forgave me too," he whispered.

"My wife. She forgave me long before I forgave myself."

Rose nodded.

"She saw you clearly. Even in your silence."

Peter exhaled shakily, a release long overdue.

"I thought I had lost everything," he said softly. "But it seems... they left me pieces of themselves. Waiting for when I was finally strong enough to hold them."

Rose rested her hand over his.

"And now you are strong enough."

He opened his eyes, meeting hers.

"For years," he said, "I carried sorrow as if it were the only proof I had loved them. But these letters... they show me something else."

"What is that?"

"That love doesn't vanish with time. It waits."

Rose nodded gently.

"And now it's found its way back to you."

CHAPTER FORTY-ONE
What Comes After

Later that evening, Peter returned to the attic chest. He placed the bundle of his wife's letters carefully beside Lily's notebook.

Two voices.

Two women.

Two versions of love he had feared he had lost forever.

But they were here, helping him rebuild the parts of himself he had abandoned.

Peter closed the chest softly.

When he turned back toward Rose, there was something steadier in his expression now. Something open.

"Thank you," he said. "For walking through this with me."

"You're not alone anymore," she replied.

"No," Peter said. "And perhaps… I never truly was."

Rose stepped beside him. Together, they looked toward the door leading to the garden, where the bulbs slept beneath fresh soil, waiting for spring.

Peter's voice was quiet but sure.

"I am ready," he said.

"For what?" Rose asked.

"For whatever grows next."

CHAPTER FORTY-TWO
The Third Rose

Morning settled softly over the garden, a pale hush of light brushing the soil they'd spent days tending. Rose came out carrying a small linen bundle, but she said nothing about its contents. Peter waited, hands clasped behind his back, watching the steam rise from the damp earth.

She knelt first, setting the bundle gently on the ground.

"I… brought these," she said quietly.

Peter lowered himself beside her. When she unfolded the cloth, two rose bulbs rolled into her palm, pale and smooth, each holding its secret shape.

She looked at him, unsure.

"I thought… maybe we could plant something for them."

Peter understood immediately, and the breath he drew was slow, steady, full of warmth and ache.

"Yes," he said. "For them."

Rose placed the first bulb in his hand.

"For your wife," she said.

Peter nodded.

He pressed it into the soil, covering it with careful fingers.

"For my Rose," he whispered. "Who loved me before I learned how to love back."

Rose handed him the second bulb.

"And for Lily," she said softly.

Peter held the bulb for a long moment before lowering it gently beside the first.

"For my daughter," he said. "Who carried more courage in her small hands than I ever found in a lifetime. Who forgave me long before I was brave enough to forgive myself."

They covered the second bulb together, palms brushing lightly.

When the earth was smooth again, Rose sat back on her heels, exhaling.

"It's beautiful," she said. "Two roses. Side by side."

She reached to fold the linen cloth, but Peter placed his hand over it before she could.

"Wait," he said.

Rose looked up, puzzled.

Peter opened a cloth he was holding,

A rose bulb rested inside. Rose blinked at it, surprised.

Peter said gently. "I bought one more."

She stared at him, not understanding.

Peter took the third bulb and held it between them.

"There are three roses in my life," he said. "I could not leave the third unplanted.

"Her breath caught, but she still didn't speak.

"For my wife," he said, nodding toward the first mound of soil.

"For my daughter," he said, touching the second.

Then he turned to her.

"And one for the Rose who came home… and carried the other two back to me."

Rose swallowed, her eyes warming with emotion that had no rush, no demand, only depth.

He smiled, small and soft.

"You carried them both back to me," he said. "I never knew I would have another chance to be anyone's family. How could I not honour you too?"

Rose lowered her gaze, overcome.
He placed the third bulb in her hand.
"Will you plant this one?" he asked.
She nodded, silent.
Together, they pressed the bulb into the earth.
Her hands trembled slightly, and Peter's steadied them.
When the soil lay smooth again, the patch held three small roses in a gentle, perfect line.
Rose leaned close to him.
"They're going to bloom beautifully," she murmured.
Peter looked at the garden, the reborn paths, the revived rosebush, the bulbs sleeping beneath the earth.
For the first time in years, the world felt like a place that could hold him gently.
"They already have," he said quietly. "In ways I never expected."
Rose slipped her arm through his.
The garden exhaled around them.
No grand declarations.
No dramatic endings.
Just two people standing in the quiet morning, watching the light fall over the earth where three roses waited to grow.
A beginning.
Small.
Tender.
True.
And enough.

EPILOGUE
The Garden of Three Roses

————————— ✦ —————————

Five years later, the garden woke before the house did. Dawn moved quietly across the cottage walls, softening the edges of the world, settling like a blessing on the beds they had tended by hand. The soil was richer now. The colours deeper. The place no longer carried the heaviness of what had been lost, but the warmth of what had grown in its place.

Peter stood at the back door, his hand resting on the frame as he looked out. His steps were slower these days, but steady. Age had gentled him more than it had weakened him. His eyes, once guarded, now held an openness he had earned through years of effort and forgiveness.

He stepped into the morning air.

The tulips they had planted together had multiplied in soft, uneven lines along the borders, blooming in shades of pink, white, and pale gold. The old rosebush, his wife's rosebush, climbed higher each year, spilling petals along the stone wall like memories finally allowed to rest.

Behind him, the door opened.

Rose stepped out with two cups of tea, her hair tucked behind one ear, her expression warm as the morning light.

"You are up early," she said, handing him his cup.

"The flowers are earlier," Peter replied. "I did not want to miss the first bloom."

They walked together to the patch they had planted that first morning of beginnings.

Three roses bloomed there now, each already touched
by sunlight:
One for Rose,
one for Lily Rose,
and one for the Rose who came home.
"This one opened before sunrise," she said, kneeling
beside the newest bloom. "Just like last year."
Peter looked down at it, his expression softening.
"She always was eager," he murmured.
Rose laughed under her breath.
"Are you talking about me or my mother?"
"Both," he said with a quiet smile.
They sat on the wooden bench they had built together
three summers earlier. The air around them carried the
scent of roses, dew, and the beginning of spring.
"You know," Rose said softly, "my mother would
have loved this garden. She would have loved seeing
you like this."
Peter breathed in slowly, letting the warmth settle in
him.
"I hope she sees it now," he said. "I hope she forgave
me fully."
Rose slipped her hand into his, a familiar gesture.
"She did," Rose said. "She forgave you long before
you forgave yourself."
They watched the morning settle over the flowers,
soft and unrushed.
"Do you ever wish things had been different?" she
asked.
Peter considered this, his eyes moving from Rose to
the garden to the light-stained sky.
"I wish I had learned earlier," he said. "But I am
grateful I learned at all."
Rose looked up at him, her eyes warm.

"She would be proud of you."
Peter let his gaze return to the three roses blooming in
their quiet line.
Each one carried a story.
Each one bore a name he carried in his heart.
"I think," he said softly, "that I am finally proud of
myself too."
A breeze drifted through the garden, rustling leaves
and petals, as if approving.
"The village has a spring market next week," Rose said
gently. "Will you come with me?"
Peter chuckled softly.
"I will. I want to see what the world looks like beyond
this gate again."
Rose leaned gently into his shoulder.
"There is still plenty left for you," she said.
Peter looked over the garden, the colours, the light,
the living things that had returned.
He had spent most of his life in shadow.
But he would end it in the light.
And the garden, blooming quietly around them,
seemed to agree.

Sequel Prologue
Where New Stories Take Root

———————◆———————

Before dawn fully claimed the sky, the garden breathed in the cool hush of another beginning. Soft gold light touched the roses first, then the tulips, then the old stone wall that had held so many seasons of memory. The cottage behind the garden looked both familiar and changed. Fresh curtains swayed in the windows. Warm colours glowed on the walls. Laughter had begun to echo through its rooms again. Inside, Rose moved quietly through the hall with a small bundle nestled in her arms. The baby stirred against her, warm and impossibly new. She opened the back door and stepped into the garden, letting the morning air settle around them.

The wooden bench stood beneath the climbing rosebush, its grain worn smooth by years of use. Peter's bench.

It waited in the shade, patient as ever.

Rose approached it slowly, her breath catching the way it always did when she saw it empty.

"I wish you were here," she whispered.

She sat down and shifted the baby in her arms. A tiny face peeked from the blanket, eyes the colour of early spring, lips forming the beginnings of a yawn. The world was only minutes old to her.

"He would have adored you," Rose said softly. "He would have read to you every evening until you fell asleep. He would have held you the way he wished he'd held your mother. And he would have planted something here, just for you."

A faint breeze moved through the garden, brushing
petals and leaves as though in agreement.
Rose lowered her voice.
"Lily," she whispered, touching the baby's cheek.
"That is your name. A name once carried by a girl
who was brave long before she understood the cost. A
girl who loved deeply, fiercely, and quietly."
The baby blinked at her, as if absorbing the story
already.
Rose stood and walked toward the flower bed Peter
had tended with such reverence.
Four blooms stood together:
One for Rose,
one for Lily Rose,
one for Thomas,
one for the Rose who came home.
But beside them, just beyond the line Peter had
planted, grew a fifth.
It had opened in the night.
Bright. Full.
As though it had been waiting for someone.
Rose knelt, balancing the baby against her shoulder.
"Look," she whispered. "A flower for you. A sign,
perhaps."
She touched the new bloom gently, its petals
trembling under her fingertips.
"Your story begins where his ended," she said to the
child. "In this garden. In this light. And maybe one
day, you will find something here that even he could
not."
The wind stirred again, warmer now, curling through
the roses with a soft murmur.

A promise.
A breath.
A doorway opening.
Rose held her daughter close, her heart full of the weight and wonder of the future.
"The world will not always be easy," she whispered. "But you come from a line of Roses. And every one of them learned how to bloom."
She stood in the morning quiet, the baby warm against her, the flowers shimmering gently in the light.
And in the garden, he rebuilt, the next chapter waited, rooted, ready, and rising toward the sun.

MEET THE AUTHOR

Rimjhim Sud builds worlds in more than one way.
By day she works in IT, structuring systems with precision and quiet discipline.
Beyond the screen, she brings celebrations to life through GoldRain Events, the company she founded with her brilliant sister – Sona, to turn moments into memories.

But between the lines of work and the glow of event lights, writing has always been her truest craft.
Her stories linger long after the last page is turned, rooted in quiet moments, unspoken emotions, and the fragile threads that bind families through love, distance, and time.

She believes the most powerful stories are the ones that bloom slowly
where healing arrives in whispers rather than declarations,

and where the smallest gestures carry the greatest
weight.

The Garden of Three Roses is her first novel, a tribute
to memory, forgiveness, and the enduring beauty
of second chances.